The Space Station

Written by Amy McCaw
Illustrated by Jorge Santillan

Miss Zebra showed the class a book about space.

Tao Meerkat said, "I want to be an astronaut!"

"You will like our class adventure then," said Miss Zebra. She opened the book.

Confident Reader titles are ideal for children who are developing greater reading confidence and stamina, and who can independently read simple stories with a wider vocabulary.

Special features:

Wider vocabulary, reinforced through repetition

Detailed pictures for added interest and discussion

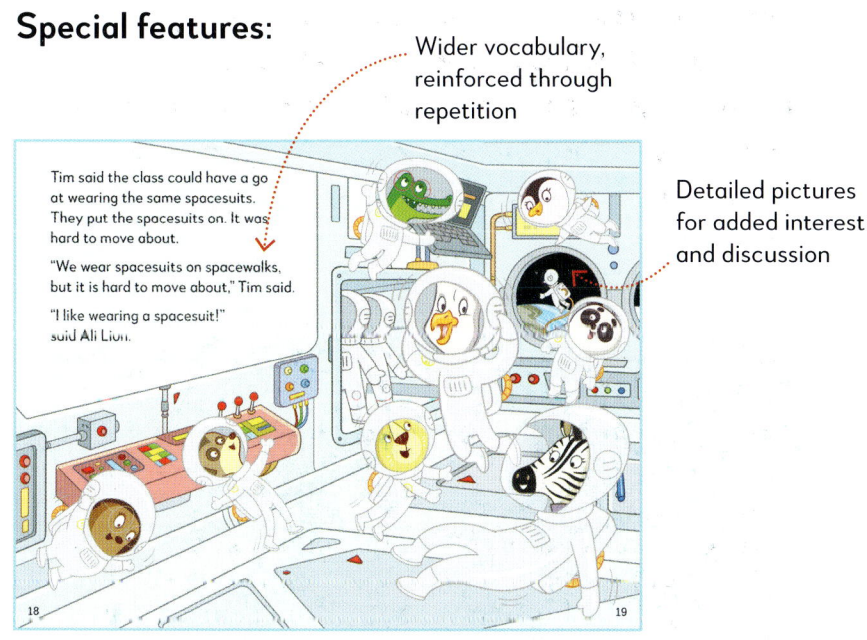

Longer sentences

Ladybird

Educational Consultant: James Clements
Subject Consultant: Stuart Atkinson
Autism Consultant: Child Autism UK
Cerebral Palsy Consultant: Pace
Book Banding Consultant: Kate Ruttle

LADYBIRD BOOKS

UK | USA | Canada | Ireland | Australia
India | New Zealand | South Africa

Ladybird Books is part of the Penguin Random House group of companies whose addresses can be found at global.penguinrandomhouse.com.

www.penguin.co.uk   www.puffin.co.uk   www.ladybird.co.uk

First published 2024
001

Written by Amy McCaw
Text copyright © Ladybird Books Ltd, 2024
Illustrations by Jorge Santillan
Illustrations copyright © Ladybird Books Ltd, 2024

The moral right of the illustrator has been asserted

Printed in China

The authorized representative in the EEA is Penguin Random House Ireland, Morrison Chambers, 32 Nassau Street, Dublin D02 YH68

A CIP catalogue record for this book is available from the British Library

ISBN: 978-0-241-56375-5

All correspondence to:
Ladybird Books
Penguin Random House Children's
One Embassy Gardens, 8 Viaduct Gardens, London SW11 7BW

Everyone saw a space station in the book.

They saw an astronaut called Tim Eagle.

Suddenly, everyone was floating around the space station.

"Floating is great!" said Tao, as he floated around. "I am so happy!"

Tim laughed. "I like floating, too!"

"Can we see the Earth?" asked Tao.

"Look through the window," said Tim.

They looked out of the window into space and saw the Earth.

An astronaut called Suri Badger came in to see Tim.

"One of our solar panels is broken," said Suri. "I will have to go on a spacewalk to repair it."

Suri put on a spacesuit. She opened a hatch and went out of the space station.

The students looked out at her through the window.

Tim said the class could have a go at wearing the same spacesuits. They put the spacesuits on. It was hard to move about.

"We wear spacesuits on spacewalks, but it is hard to move about," Tim said.

"I like wearing a spacesuit!" said Ali Lion.

"Can we see where astronauts sleep?" asked Tao.

Tim showed the students where a sleeping bag was. "The sleeping bags are tied to the space station so we don't float around," said Tim.

"Can we see what astronauts eat?" asked Ali.

"We eat the same food as on Earth and some freeze-dried food, too. Our plates are tied down so they don't float away and get broken," said Tim.

Ali and Tao tasted some freeze-dried food from the plates.

"I like space food!" said Tao.

"Look, everyone!" said Tim.

They looked out of the window and saw Suri. She was repairing the broken solar panel.

Suddenly, Suri's spanner slipped out of her hand. It floated away and got stuck between the panels.

"I am too big to get it," said Suri.

"I can get the spanner," said Tao. "I want to go on a spacewalk."

Suri opened the hatch. Tao was so happy to see the Earth from space.

It was time to get the spanner, but it was hard to reach.

Tao reached out his hand . . .

. . . and slipped off the platform! Tao could have floated off, but he was tied to the space station.

Tao got back on the platform. He reached out and got the spanner that was stuck between the solar panels. He gave it to Suri. Suri was happy!

Suri repaired the solar panel.

Then, they went back into the space station.

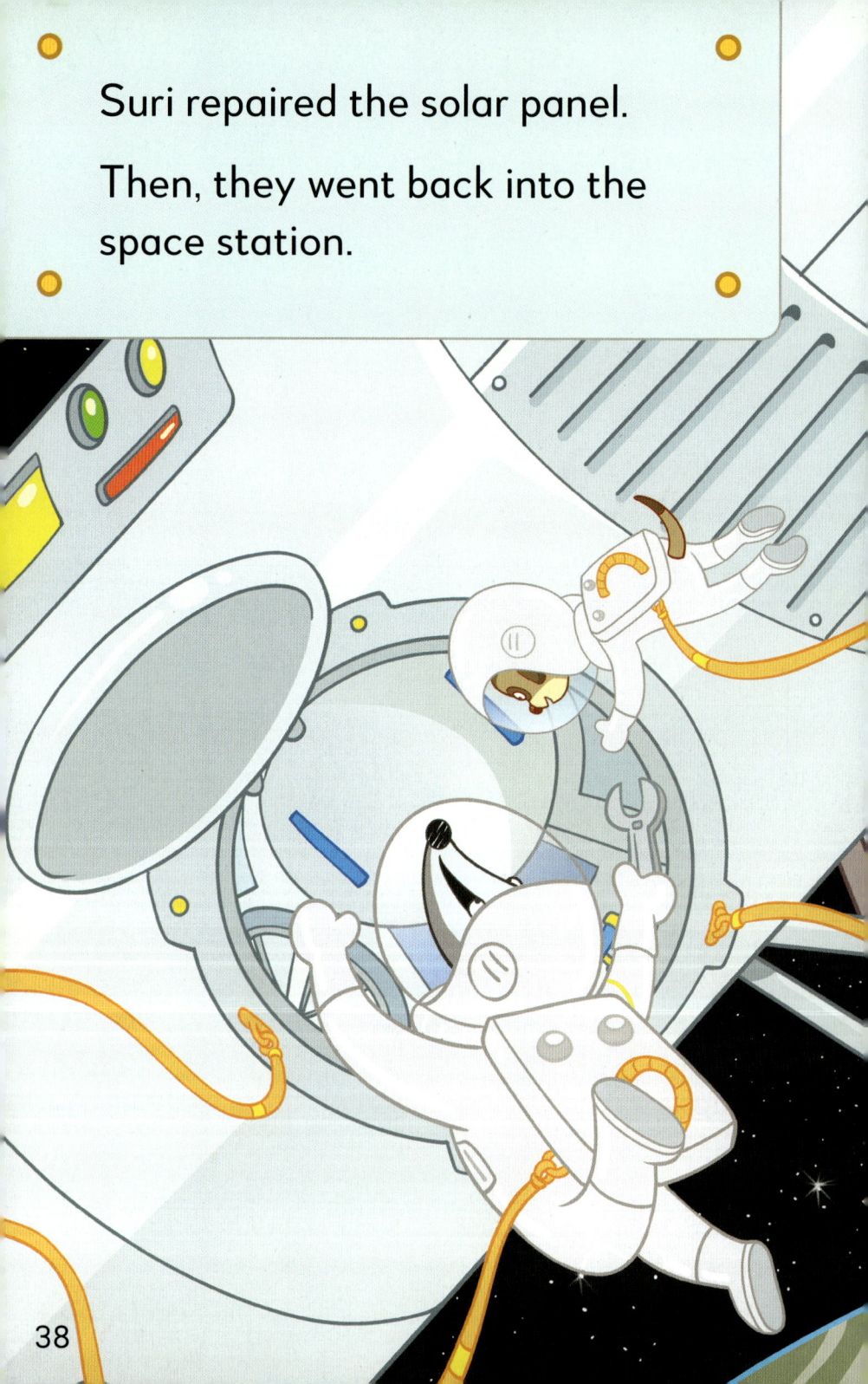

Everyone was happy as Tao and Suri came back into the space station.

"One day, I want to be an astronaut like Suri," Tao said.

"What an adventure! You will be a great astronaut one day!" said Suri.

Tim gave the class some freeze-dried ice cream to taste. The ice cream slipped out of Ali's hand, and it floated away. Everyone laughed. Then, it was time to go.

Miss Zebra put away the book. "What a big adventure on the space station!"

Tao looked at his space station. One day, he wanted to go back to space.

How much do you remember about the story of *The Space Station*? Answer these questions and find out!

- Which student wants to be an astronaut?
- Why does Suri Badger go outside the space station?
- Why are sleeping bags attached to the space station?
- What happens when Tao Meerkat slips off the platform?
- What happens to Ali Lion's ice cream?